April 2004

Eight Authors.
Eight Stories.
One Ending.
Yours.
End of Story.

C O N G R A T U L A T I O N S ! You've found
a limited edition BBC Three End of Story book.
It could change your life.

In this book you'll find eight unfinished short stories
from some of the world's best-selling authors.

They all need an ending. Can you write it?

BBC Three's End Of Story invites you to pick a tale
and finish what's already been started, in fewer than
1200 words. No struggling for that opening line.

Your entry will be judged by a team of professional
readers. Make the final three, and you get to meet
the power players of the literary world and your
chosen author.

Be the best and it could be the start of a new career.
You'll be published online, and receive a priceless
hand-made book of your winning entry.

You can enter only once, so pick your author and
genre wisely. The deadline is the 31st May 2004,
so there's no time for writer's block.

Go to the back of the book for all you need to know
or visit the website:

www.bbc.co.uk/endofstory.

It's as simple as that.

End of Story.

This book is published to accompany the BBC Three television series and short story writing competition "End Of Story."

Series Producer of "End Of Story." is Alison Black.

Thanks to Emma Shackleton, Tracey Smith, and John Martin at BBC Books.

Published by "End Of Story."
BBC Scotland
Queen Margaret Drive
Glasgow
G12 8DG
First published 2004.

ISBN: 0 563 52196 1

Commissioning Editor: Stuart Murphy

Project Editors: Esther Coleman-Hawkins and Mari Steven

Designer: ISO, Glasgow

Text set in Century Schoolbook

Printed and bound in Great Britain by **Martins The Printers Ltd**

"End Of Story." Official Web Site **www.bbc.co.uk/endofstory**

Contents

Billy Bone

by Ian Rankin

Ian Rankin was born in the Kingdom of Fife in 1960. His first Rebus novel, Knots and Crosses, *was published in 1987, and the Rebus books are now translated into twenty-two languages and are bestsellers on several continents. His most recent novel,* Resurrection Men, *was a Sunday Times Number One bestseller. A contributor to BBC Two's 'Newsnight Review', he also presented his own TV series, 'Ian Rankin's Evil Thoughts', on Channel 4 in 2002.*

He recently received the OBE for services to literature, opting to receive the prize in his home city of Edinburgh, where he lives with his partner and two sons.

HIS NAME WAS BILLY BONE, and he was lying in a hedge, nose bleeding, mouth open so he could take gasps of breath through broken teeth. There was a pain in his chest and a dull ache in both legs. The impact had thrown him a good twelve or fifteen feet, contact with the hedge grazing what bits of him had been left intact by the car. There were thorns piercing his clothing, and one of his shoes was missing, the cold air numbing his toes. At least he was wearing new socks: some of the pairs back home had holes in them. Clean underwear, too, now that he thought of it. They always said that, didn't they? If you're going to be hit by a vehicle, make sure you're wearing clean pants. The screech of brakes had brought faces to windows, and then the owners of those faces to their doors. The driver had stopped. Billy could hear the car's engine idling. Must've been doing seventy, the sod. In a suburban street, kids and schools. Mind you, most of the younger kids would be tucked up in bed by now. Midnight when he'd left the pub, one of the last to finish his drink. Gerry, the long-time barman, always eyed him warily if he stuck around to the death. Tonight, Billy had taken his empty pint glass up to the bar, placed it on one of the drip-trays.

"It's all right, Gerry", he'd said. " I'm not hanging about to do you over". Said it with a wink, because one time, a few years back, that's pretty much what he had done. Not on his own turf, of course: over in Fife. Problem was, he'd spent the evening casing the place, which meant not looking suspicious, which in turn meant drinking. Six or seven pints he'd nursed, and by the time he was the last customer left in the place, his threat to the barman had come out slurred, so that he'd had to repeat himself. And then the barman – a young Aussie – had turned out to have a few moves of his own. Quicker reflexes than Billy and with arms stronger than they looked. Six months he'd done for that, the judge having a good old dig at him. Not his first offence by any means, but one which "smacked of incompetence as much as despair". Which was the reason Gerry wasn't keen on him lingering after last orders.

"Where does it hurt?" a voice was asking him. He could hear the buttons on a mobile phone being pressed. It was a woman doing the asking. He'd seen her face before: about thirty seconds before, the other side of the windscreen from him. Passenger, she'd been. The driver was a young man, holding the mobile to his ear as he called for an ambulance.

"You could've killed me," Billy told the woman.

"You just sort of stumbled off the pavement," she replied.

"Speed your boy-racer friend was doing, I could be dead."

"I was hardly touching twenty," the man said, before giving their location to whoever was on the other end of the phone.

"Seventy, easy," Billy argued, feeling the pain again in his chest. "Think I've got a punctured lung."

The woman looked worried, turned to her boyfriend. "Gareth, tell them to hurry."

Other figures were approaching. Passers-by, people from the houses.

"It's Billy Bone," someone said. "Hey, Billy, you all right?"

"Crashed into me... can't breathe."

"Want me to phone one of them lawyers off the telly? Accident claims and all that?"

"He fell off the pavement," the woman passenger stressed.

"Tell that to the jury, missus," the voice said with a laugh.

The street lights started to fade as Billy Bone felt himself drifting away. His last thought was: Christ, am I dying here or what...?

He spent six days in hospital, and five weeks convalescing at home. Wore a neck-brace for the first week, filling in forms for a compensation claim. Two dental appointments to cap his broken teeth. Turned out the driver was a teacher at the local high school, his girlfriend the school secretary. Both of them sober, returning home from her mum's house. Not rich then, which had seemed to disappoint the half-dozen lawyers Billy had spoken to. Some of them, he got their phone number from the TV adverts, just as the bystander had suggested; others, he found in the Yellow Pages. A couple were keen to take up his case, at least initially, but now he found himself leaving messages whenever he phoned them – costing him a fortune too, which he always pointed out to the receptionist. And him not earning.

Well, not 'earning' earning. He still had the Social, but all his other wee jobs had been somewhat curtailed, partly because he didn't want any private detectives getting shots of him while he was still up and about – just in case Gareth the driver had any suspicions. At the same time he was soon sick of lying on the sofa. He'd venture out with the aid of a stick (borrowed from Mrs Johnson along the landing – her husband had died a year past, no use her hanging onto his old walking-stick), get as far as the local shops and the pub. Gerry would look at the stick and shake his head.

"Two broken ribs," Billy would remind him. "Whiplash and a fractured pelvis."

"Whatever you say, Billy."

And then one day, while he was watching daytime TV, the doorbell rang. It was a Detective Constable called Haston. Billy recognised him immediately.

"What do you want?" he asked.

"Don't worry, I'm not coming in." Despite which, Haston peered over Billy's shoulder, as if to size up any criminal activity beyond. "Just got a bit of news for you."

"Oh aye?" Billy's eyes narrowed. Haston and him went back a ways; no chance of this being good news.

"We won't be charging Gareth Ellis. His version's checked out…"

"But he near killed me."

"Then you should be a bit more careful."

"He was doing seventy."

But Haston was shaking his head. "Between twenty-five and twenty-eight, according to the tests."

"What tests?"

"All that rubber he left on the road when he hit the brakes: it gives us an idea of the speed he was doing. So does the distance you were thrown."

Haston slid his hands into his pockets. "Twenty-eight's maybe a bit high for a built-up area, but within the speed limit. No drugs or alcohol in his system, and his passenger backs up his story. You just fell off the kerb, Billy."

"I don't believe I'm hearing this." Billy leaned against the edge of the door. "He put me in hospital."

"Six pints of Best put you in hospital, Billy. Now about

that other thing..."

"What other thing?"

Haston smiled a cold smile. "That watch we found in your pocket."

"Illegal search, that was," Billy snapped. "My lawyer's solid on that."

"Maybe so, but the watch was stolen, Billy. And you still haven't explained how you came by it."

"I have."

"What? Our old friend the 'mysterious stranger'? A tenner changing hands in a pub, only you can't remember which one or what he looked like?" The smile was still there. "How many times you been done for housebreaking, Billy? I'm starting to lose count."

"I can't believe you're doing this!" Billy's anger was as real as it was sudden. "I'm the victim here!"

"Well..." Haston examined the tips of his shoes. "Now you know how it feels, eh?"

Billy went to say something, but thought better of it and slammed shut the door instead. He watched the letter-box, and sure enough it opened. Haston's voice coming from it.

"We'll be following up on that watch, Billy. Few more items were taken at the same time, if your mysterious stranger should have anything he wants you to buy." The flap clapped shut.

Billy went back to the sofa, but couldn't sit still, could

hardly think straight. He paced the living-room, rubbing his neck and forehead. If there was no liability... no one to pin the blame on...well, those law firms would drop his claim. No money, no comp for everything he'd gone through. He kicked the walking-stick as he passed it, sent it clattering against the wall. It wasn't fair, none of it. They were all ganging up on him, same as ever. All because he was the one with previouses. So it had to be his fault. Couldn't be that nice teacher and his nice girlfriend. Lying couple of tossers. Billy paused in his pacing, checked the time on the video. Knew what he had to do.

The school was only a ten-minute walk away. The bell for the end of day was ringing as Billy reached the gates. He reckoned he would recognise the car: there'd been a picture of it in the local paper. Black and white photo, but he reckoned he'd know it. He'd know the faces. Kids walked past him as if he didn't exist, too busy shouting and running, or with their eyes fixed on the pavement. A blue estate car was first out of the gates, but that wasn't it. Five more cars passed him, some of the drivers staring at him in suspicion, and then he saw it. Saw the same two faces. And he stepped into the road.

Gareth Ellis sounded the horn, but Billy stood his ground. The girlfriend had recognised him: she turned and said something which caused Ellis's eyes to widen. He tried the horn again, but Billy just smiled.

The girlfriend had her mobile out, but Ellis was shaking his head. The driver's-side door opened and the two men were face to face for the first time since that night: sods hadn't even bothered visiting the hospital. Canny move though, in retrospect: might have hinted they felt guilty otherwise.

"Can you get out of the way, please?"

A crowd of kids had gathered, knowing something wasn't right. Billy winked at one of them, then raised his right arm and pointed at Ellis.

"You're going to die. You're going to rot away and die, just you wait."

The girlfriend's voice: "Gareth, let me phone the police" But Gareth Ellis's eyes were on Billy.

"Take it from me," Billy went on. "Nobody's going to be able to stop it. Nothing you can do about it."

"Are you threatening me?"

"Just stating a simple fact." Billy had taken a couple of steps forward, finger still pointing. At the last moment, Ellis ducked, but Billy's finger had touched his forehead, right at the spot between his eyes. Some of the onlookers were laughing, others calling out for the fight to start. The girlfriend was punching numbers into her phone. Ellis was back in the driver's seat, closing the door, putting the car into reverse. After a few yards he turned to see what Billy was up to. Billy had brought the same finger to his lips, and now blew across its tip, as if blowing smoke from the barrel of a gun.

"Is that you claiming him, mister?" one of the kids asked.

"More in the way of a curse, son," Billy answered. "But it means he's a marked man, all right."

Almost a year later, Detective Constable Mark Haston thought back on the scene as he sat in the undertaker's office. He was wearing a dark suit, crisp white shirt, thin black tie. He was staring into space, not really aware of his surroundings. Over a dozen witnesses had heard Billy Bone's threat. Except that it hadn't been a "threat" as such. As Bone himself had put it, it had been a curse.

Nevertheless, within the month, Gareth Ellis had been dead. An unspotted tumour; a shock to family and friends. And cause for Haston once more to visit Billy Bone's flat. But there was nothing to be done. As the doctors had said, Bone hadn't given the teacher the brain tumour. Nobody had, with the possible exceptions of God or the Devil.

And eventually, Haston had let the matter drop. It wasn't against the law to curse someone, to lay a fingertip against their forehead. Mark it down to bad luck or coincidence or anything else you liked. Centuries back, Bone might have been treated differently: tried as a warlock, perhaps. But this was the twenty-first century. People didn't just die because you laid a curse on them.

Haston had pressed for an additional autopsy. He wanted to be sure Ellis hadn't been attacked or poisoned. The pathologist had sought to reassure him. Other cases came along – proper cases – and Haston pushed it to the back of his mind. Billy Bone hadn't been in trouble since then, and no one else had died. Simple coincidence. But now someone had died. She was lying in a coffin somewhere on those very premises. Haston's own daughter. Thirteen years old and being driven home by her boyfriend's father when the car had been hit side-on by a stolen Volkswagen Golf. The joy-rider suffering only bruising and concussion; Haston's daughter the only fatality. Her boyfriend's father suffered whiplash and a broken collar-bone. She'd just finished fastening her seat-belt when the Golf flew out across the junction and smashed into her door.

The driver fifteen, with a previous record for car theft – joy-riding they called it, but where was the joy? And every time he broke the law, they slapped his wrists. Even now, he might well escape a custodial sentence. Even if he did go away, it wouldn't be for long. He'd learn no lesson. And Gillian would still be dead. No bringing her back. Haston's wife at home in their darkened bedroom, turned towards the wall, weeping and reaching for the pill-bottle.

Where was the fairness in any of it? To all intents, it was murder, yet that wasn't how the law would see it. Reckless endangerment: not even manslaughter. People got off all the time with crimes just like it. Mishaps and errors and accidents. The wrong place at the wrong time: ten seconds either way and nothing would have happened… not to his family at any rate: maybe to someone else's.

It didn't explain the why. That huge, cruel question. He thought back to hit-and-runs he'd worked on, accident scenes he'd experienced. And then Billy Bone had swum up to the surface. Billy Bone's finger outstretched. Billy Bone, whose curse had worked once. And if once, why not again?

What happens next? Over to you…

Dryad
by Joanne Harris

Joanne Harris was born in Yorkshire in 1964, the daughter of a French mother and an English father. She was a French teacher at a boys' grammar school in Leeds when her first novel, The Evil Seed, *was published in 1989. Since then she has written* Sleep, Pale Sister, *the Whitbread-shortlisted* Chocolat *(now a major film),* Blackberry Wine, Five Quarters of the Orange, Coastliners, *and* Holy Fools. *She has also written a cookery book,* The French Kitchen, *with Fran Warde. Her first collection of short stories,* "Jigs & Reels," *has just been published.*

Joanne Harris gave up teaching four years ago to write full-time and lives with her husband and young daughter in Yorkshire.

IN A QUIET LITTLE CORNER of the Botanical Gardens, between a stand of old trees and a thick holly hedge, there is a small green metal bench. Almost invisible against the greenery, few people use it, for it catches no sun and offers only a partial view of the lawns. A plaque in the centre reads: In Memory of Josephine Morgan Clarke, 1912-1989. I should know – I put it there – and yet I hardly knew her, hardly noticed her, except for that one rainy Spring day when our paths crossed and we almost became friends.

I was twenty-five, pregnant and on the brink of divorce. Five years earlier, life had seemed an endless passage of open doors; now I could hear them clanging shut, one by one; marriage; job; dreams. My one pleasure was the Botanical Gardens; its mossy paths; its tangled walkways, its quiet avenues of oaks and lindens. It became my refuge, and when David was at work (which was almost all the time) I walked there, enjoying the scent of cut grass and the play of light through the tree branches. It was surprisingly quiet; I noticed few other visitors, and was glad of it. There was one exception, however; an elderly lady in a dark coat who always sat on the same bench under the trees, sketching. In rainy weather, she brought an umbrella: on sunny days, a hat. That was Josephine Clarke; and twenty-five years later, with one daughter married and the other still at school, I have never forgotten her, or the story she told me of her first and only love.

It had been a bad morning. David had left on a quarrel (again), drinking his coffee without a word before leaving for the office in the rain. I was tired and lumpish in my pregnancy clothes; the kitchen needed cleaning; there was nothing on TV and everything in the world seemed to have gone yellow around the edges, like the pages of a newspaper that has been read and re-read until there's nothing new left inside. By midday I'd had enough; the rain had stopped, and I set off for the Gardens; but I'd hardly gone in through the big wrought-iron gate when it began again – great billowing sheets of it – so that I ran for the shelter of the nearest tree, under which Mrs Clarke was already sitting.

We sat on the bench side-by-side, she calmly busy with her sketchbook, I watching the tiresome rain with the slight embarrassment that enforced proximity to a stranger often brings. I could not help but glance at the sketchbook – furtively, like reading someone else's newspaper on the Tube – and I saw that the page was covered with studies of trees. One tree, in fact, as I looked more closely; our tree – a beech – its young leaves shivering in the rain. She had drawn it in soft, chalky green pencil, and her hand was sure and delicate, managing to convey the texture of the bark as well as the strength of the tall, straight trunk and the movement of the leaves. She caught me looking, and I apologised.

"That's all right, dear," said Mrs Clarke. "You take a look, if you'd like to." And she handed me the book.

Politely, I took it. I didn't really want to; I wanted to be alone; I wanted the rain to stop; I didn't want a conversation with an old lady about her drawings. And yet they were wonderful drawings – even I could see that, and I'm no expert – graceful, textured, economical. She had devoted one page to leaves; one to bark; one to the tender cleft where branch meets trunk and the grain of the bark coarsens before smoothing out again as the limb performs its graceful arabesque into the leaf canopy. There were winter branches; summer foliage; shoots and roots and wind-shaken leaves. There must have been fifty pages of studies; all beautiful, and all, I saw, of the same tree.

I looked up to see her watching me. She had very bright eyes, bright and brown and curious; and there was a curious smile on her small, vivid face as she took back her sketchbook and said: "Piece of work, isn't he?"

It took me some moments to understand that she was referring to the tree.

"I've always had a soft spot for the beeches," continued Mrs Clarke, "ever since I was a little girl. Not all trees are so friendly; and some of them – the oaks and the cedars especially – can be quite antagonistic to human beings. It's not really their fault; after all, if you'd been persecuted for as long as they have, I imagine you'd be entitled to feel some racial hostility, wouldn't you?" And she smiled at me, poor old dear, and I looked nervously at the rain and wondered whether I should risk making a dash for the bus shelter. But she seemed quite harmless, so I smiled back and nodded, hoping that was enough.

"That's why I don't like this kind of thing," said Mrs Clarke, indicating the bench on which we were sitting. "This wooden bench under this living tree – all our history of chopping and burning. My husband was a carpenter. He never did understand about trees. To him, it was all about product – floorboards and furniture. They don't feel, he used to say. I mean, how could anyone live with stupidity like that?"

She laughed and ran her fingertips tenderly along the edge of her sketchbook. "Of course I was young; in those days a girl left home; got married; had children; it was expected. If you didn't, there was something wrong with you. And that's how I found myself up the duff at twenty-two, married – to Stan Clarke, of all people – and living in a two-up, two-down off the Station Road and wondering; is this it? Is this all?"

That was when I should have left. To hell with politeness; to hell with the rain. But she was telling my story as well as her own, and I could feel the echo down the lonely passages of my heart. I nodded without knowing it, and her bright brown eyes flicked to mine with sympathy and unexpected humour.

"Well, we all find our little comforts where we can," she said, shrugging. "Stan didn't know it, and what you don't know doesn't hurt, right? But Stanley never had much of an imagination. Besides, you'd never have thought it to look at me. I kept house; I worked hard; I raised my boy – and nobody guessed about my fella next door, and the hours we spent together."

She looked at me again, and her vivid face broke into a smile of a thousand wrinkles. "Oh yes, I had my fella," she said. "And he was everything a man should be. Tall; silent; certain; strong. Sexy – and how! Sometimes when he was naked I could hardly bear to look at him, he was so beautiful. The only thing was – he wasn't a man at all."

Mrs Clarke sighed, and ran her hands once more across the pages of her sketchbook. "By rights," she went on, "he wasn't even a he. Trees have no gender – not in English, anyway – but they do have identity. Oaks are masculine, with their deep roots and resentful natures. Birches are flighty and feminine; so are hawthorns and cherry trees. But my fella was a beech, a copper beech; red-headed in autumn, veering to the most astonishing shades of purple-green in spring. His skin was pale and smooth; his limbs a dancer's; his body straight and slim and powerful. Dull weather made him sombre, but in sunlight he shone like a Tiffany lampshade, all harlequin bronze and sun-dappled rose, and if you stood underneath his branches you could hear the ocean in the leaves. He stood at the bottom of our little bit of garden, so that he was the last thing I saw when I went to bed, and the first thing I saw when I got up in the morning; and on some days I swear the only reason I got up at all was the knowledge that he'd be there waiting for me, outlined and strutting against the peacock sky.

Year by year, I learned his ways. Trees live slowly, and long. A year of mine was only a day to him; and I taught myself to be patient, to converse over months rather than minutes, years rather than days. I'd always been good at drawing – although Stan always said it was a waste of time – and now I drew the beech (or The Beech, as he had become to me) again and again, winter into summer and back again, with a lover's devotion to detail. Gradually I became obsessed – with his form; his intoxicating beauty; the long and complex language of leaf and shoot. In summer he spoke to me with his branches; in winter I whispered my secrets to his sleeping roots.

You know, trees are the most restful and contemplative of living things. We ourselves were never meant to live at this frantic speed; scurrying about in endless pursuit of the next thing, and the next; running like laboratory rats down a series of mazes towards the inevitable; snapping up our bitter treats as we go. The trees are different. Among trees I find that my breathing slows; I am conscious of my heart beating; of the world around me moving in harmony; of oceans that I have never seen; never will see. The Beech was never anxious; never in a rage, never too busy to watch or listen. Others might be petty; deceitful; cruel, unfair – but not The Beech.

The Beech was always there, always himself. And as

the years passed and I began to depend more and more on the calm serenity his presence gave me, I became increasingly repelled by the sweaty pink lab rats with their nasty ways, and I was drawn, slowly and inevitably, to the trees.

Even so, it took me a long time to understand the intensity of those feelings. In those days it was hard enough to admit to loving a black man – or worse still, a woman – but this aberration of mine – there wasn't even anything about it in the Bible, which suggested to me that perhaps I was unique in my perversity, and that even Deuteronomy had overlooked the possibility of non-mammalian, inter-species romance.

And so for more than ten years I pretended to myself that it wasn't love. But as time passed my obsession grew; I spent most of my time outdoors, sketching; my boy Daniel took his first steps in the shadow of The Beech; and on warm summer nights I would creep outside, barefoot and in my nightdress, while upstairs Stan snored fit to wake the dead, and I would put my arms around the hard, living body of my beloved and hold him close beneath the cavorting stars.

It wasn't always easy, keeping it secret. Stan wasn't what you'd call imaginative, but he was suspicious, and he must have sensed some kind of deception. He had never really liked my drawing, and now he seemed almost resentful of my little hobby, as if he saw something in my studies of trees that made him uncomfortable. The years had not improved Stan. He had been a shy young man in the days of our courtship; not bright; and awkward in the manner of one who has always been happiest working with his hands. Now he was sour – old before his time. It was only in his workshop that he really came to life. He was an excellent craftsman, and he was generous with his work, but my years alongside The Beech had given me a different perspective on carpentry, and I accepted Stan's offerings – fruitwood bowls, coffee-tables, little cabinets, all highly polished and beautifully-made – with concealed impatience and growing distaste.

And now, worse still, he was talking about moving house; of getting a nice little semi, he said, with a garden, not just a big old tree and a patch of lawn. We could afford it; there'd be space for Dan to play; and though I shook my head and refused to discuss it, it was then that the first brochures began to appear around the house, silently, like spring crocuses, promising en-suite bathrooms and inglenook fireplaces and integral garages and gas fired central heating. I had to admit, it sounded quite nice. But to leave The Beech was unthinkable. I had become dependent on him. I knew him; and I had come to believe that he knew me, needed and cared for me in a way as yet unknown among his proud and ancient kind.

Perhaps it was my anxiety that gave me away. Perhaps I under-estimated Stan, who had always been so practical, and who always snored so loudly as I crept out into the garden. All I know is that one night when I returned, exhilarated by the dark and the stars and the wind in the branches, my hair wild and my feet scuffed with green moss, he was waiting.

"You've got a fella, haven't you?"

I made no attempt to deny it; in fact, it was almost a relief to admit it to myself. To those of our generation, divorce was a shameful thing; an admission of failure. There would be a court case; Stanley would fight; Daniel would be dragged into the mess and all our friends would take Stanley's side and speculate vainly on the identity of my mysterious lover. And yet I faced it; accepted it; and in my heart a bird was singing so hard that it was all I could do not to burst out laughing.

"You have, haven't you?" Stan's face looked like a rotten apple; his eyes shone through with pinhead intensity.

"Who is it?"

What happens next? Over to you...

Imitating Katherine Walker

by Alexei Sayle

Alexei Sayle is a comedian, actor, presenter and writer. His television work as a writer and performer includes 'The Young Ones', 'Alexei Sayle's Stuff' and the 'All New Alexei Sayle Show'. He has written regularly for the Observer, Independent, Time Out, Car Magazine and Esquire and he has appeared in numerous films, from 'Indiana Jones and the Last Crusade' to 'Gorky Park' and 'Swing'. He has written two short story collections, "Barcelona Plates" and "The Dog Catcher" and a novel, Overtaken.

Alexei lives in London.

RORY SUDDENLY REALISED it had been over a month and Katherine Walker hadn't had her period yet, so obviously he needed to buy some Tampax for her. At lunchtime he got the bus right across to West London and bought an overpriced box in a Korean supermarket. When he got back to Katherine's room he opened the box and left it open on her bedside table: she would not be the sort of girl who'd hide such things away. Then the thought struck him, "Why would she leave a full box open on her bedside table?" So he had to take some out; but then immediately another thought struck him, "How many of these things did women get through in a…what would you call it, 'a session'?"

In the end, after much thought, he removed four of the things from the box then rode another bus right across to East London and left them in four separate litter bins. This took a considerable time since litter bins – unlike massive piles of litter – were few and far between right across East London.

When Rory got back to his flat it was late, he hadn't

got any work done and he'd spent most of the day carrying sanitary towels around on public transport. Rory sat on the couch, put his head in his hands and wondered how he'd got into this situation. Where could you say it had started to go wrong? Six weeks ago he certainly hadn't felt like this, a month and a half ago he'd been optimistic and happy with a feeling that he was finally getting back on his feet after so many hard times.

From 1984 to the mid 90s he'd been a wealthy man, often appearing on 'The Money Programme,' or 'Channel 4 News', being interviewed about the massively successful business that he owned called 'The Classic Car Phone Company'. At the time when he'd had the idea for it he'd been a small-time publisher and the owner of one of the very first carphones, its bulky works built into the boot of his MG Montego. It had occurred to Rory one day that people who owned classic cars like E-Type Jaguars, Gullwing Mercedes SLs, Bentley Coupes, Porsche 356s, were forced to have the same mobile phones as everyone else, their angular modern 80s plastic lines clashing with the more curvaceous, leather and wood-clad interiors of their vehicles. Rory's inspiration was to begin manufacturing a range of car phones that matched the insides of these classic cars: Bakelite handsets in place of plastic, chromed dials in place of push buttons, cloth wire in place of black cable. Soon the business expanded and he was making all kinds of things that didn't look like themselves: personal computers disguised as spindly Regency writing desks, CCTV cameras built into wrought iron lanterns to guard the gateways of converted Victorian warehouses and gilt rococo microwave cookers for the kitchens of Jewish homes in North London.

All was well until the internet boom of the late 90s. Making the mistake of thinking (as many powerful people do) that because he was good at one thing he was good at every thing, Rory invested all his money and some that wasn't his in a web site called 'mybums.com'. Now when he reflected on it he couldn't properly recall exactly what service 'mybum.com' purported to offer the internet user. Indeed now he wasn't entirely sure that anybody involved had the slightest idea what it was the site was supposed to do, apart from produce money like a mountain spring just by dint of its being a website. This supposition turned out not to be true.

His partner Jenny had taken the bankruptcy and the loss of their home quite hard but she had never openly blamed him for his idiotic greed and he was grateful for that. When they managed to obtain the tiny two bedroomed housing association flat on a quiet street south of Kings Cross she stopped crying all the time and occasionally even managed a shy smile.

This tranquil period lasted until Byron and Danuta came to stay. Byron had been Rory's closest friend at University but while Rory had gone into business Byron never settled. Rory liked to think of the other man as his wilder alter ego, travelling the world, living with the Mud Men of Papua New Guinea, getting into fights in a bar in Vietnam, being the gigolo of an aged poetess in Helsinki. For the last four years, according to the occasional curt email, he had been working in Somalia for a Spanish medical charity called 'Medicos Sin Sombreros' (Doctors Without Hats) but over a fizzing phone line from Mogadishu Byron had yelled, "Rory mate I'm coming back to London, OK to crash for a while at your place?"

"Of course mate," replied Rory. "You know we don't have the money we once had, I mean the spare room is pretty small but yeah sure..."

"Don't worry. The old lady'll be cool?"

"The old lady'll be well cool."

"Great mate, see you next Tuesday then."

*****

During the intervening period between the phone call and Byron's arrival Rory spent many hours daydreaming about what it would be like to have his closest friend living with him. When they greeted Byron at the arrivals gate at Heathrow carrying a big funny sign saying 'Lord Byron' they found he had brought back with him from Somalia, a tropical disease which made him a ghastly yellow colour, six very big suitcases and an extremely bad-tempered Croatian woman called Danuta.

As Rory's battered Volvo estate turned into their

street they passed on the left a little petting zoo attached to a children's playground, behind whose iron railings overindulged sheep grazed.

"What sort of sheep are those?" asked Danuta, who'd been silent the whole length of the A40, from the passenger seat.

"Ooh, I don't really know," said Jenny.

Danuta swore in Croatian then said mockingly, "Dey don't know what sheep it is dat live round de corner from dem… dey are idiots not to know what kind of sheep it is."

"So what kind are they Danuta?" asked Rory in a friendly, enquiring voice.

"I don't fucking know!" she shouted, "but then they aren't my fucking sheep are they you cretin?"

"I was only…" stuttered Rory before Byron cut across him, "Hey just lay off her mate alright? She's had a tough time OK?"

"Yeah, sure, I'm sorry," said Rory, aware that Jenny in the back seat was giving him a look which implied he was a weak-willed weasel even though he could only see one of her eyes under the enormous suitcase that was slowly crushing her.

As soon as they arrived Byron and Danuta immediately went to bed in the spare room where they had a noisy argument followed by very noisy sex while Rory and Jenny hauled their suitcases up the four flights of stairs.

The two travellers emerged at one in the morning, woke their hosts up and forced them to cook a huge meal which they ate without stopping smoking. Byron and Danuta had brought with them twenty cartons of a brand of Somalian cigarettes called 'Monkey Priest' which they smoked constantly, so that acrid grey clouds soon hung in the kitchen like low mist over a swamp.

Over the meal Byron told them, food spilling from his mouth, how everything was better in Somalia and how the lives of Rory and Jenny lacked spirituality, then he read them extracts from his poetry and showed them drawings he'd done of Danuta seen from the back, kneeling exposed and naked with her behind up in the air.

*****

During the next couple of weeks Rory and Jenny endured strange smells in their toilet, violent arguments between their guests followed by even more violent making-up and a deluge of insults from Danuta concerning their ignorance of different types of sheep until one day Jenny suddenly said, "Rory I can't take any more of this."

"I know darling," he replied "I'll see to it."

"Byron mate," Rory said when the couple got back from the swimming baths, "sorry but we need the spare room back. Katherine Walker, Jenny's best mate from school's coming to stay, she's just split up with her boyfriend so you know..."

Rory had been expecting some strong resistance from Byron but rather sweetly his best friend said, "Sure mate, if the chick's in trouble. Me and Danu will check into one of those Bed and Breakfast places in Argyle Square. Only thing is I'll have to leave our suitcases in the spare room 'cos I'll need to get at my poems and notebooks, change of clothes and stuff."

Rory was so relieved at Byron's easy acquiescence that he readily agreed to him leaving his luggage behind. It took him a while to realise that if Byron was going to be visiting the spare room often then he would have to fake Katherine Walker's presence in that room.

At first he approached this task with enthusiasm: he got some Prada shoes Jenny had bought at Milan airport that were far too small for her and threw them on the floor, he got the two red silk Agent Provocateur bra and pants sets his partner had always refused to have anything to do with and lay them on a chair, he found a small stylish leather suitcase left over from their wealthy days at the back of their wardrobe and put in it other T shirts, jeans and tops that Jenny had grown too fat to wear. Then he happily stood back to look at his work and felt immediately deflated; he realised it was surprisingly difficult to get a sense of somebody's absent presence. At the moment it was just an empty room with some stuff in it, there was no hint of Katherine Walker's personality.

He went into the living room and took down 'Anna Karenina' (a book he'd meant to read) from the bookshelf and laid it open at Page 49 on the table beside the bed. Next he picked up a glass and half-filled it with water, got some old scarlet lipstick of Jen's from her makeup box and with a strange tingling sensation in his calves smeared it on his own lips then took a sip and placed the glass also on the bedside table next to the book. Finally he sprayed the last of Jenny's 'Very Valentino' in the air. Again he stepped back and felt, with a deep sense of satisfaction that now Katherine Walker's personality was beginning to emerge. You could see that here was a bright, intelligent woman who wasn't afraid to look good; she liked sexy shoes, saucy underwear and vibrant lipstick. As he closed the door Rory felt a strong pang of regret that Katherine Walker wasn't really staying in their spare room.

"I see the chick's reading Tolstoy," said Byron after his first visit to his luggage.

"That's right," replied Rory, "she's a really clever woman, good-looking too."

"I'd love to know what she thinks about Anna."

"I'll ask her mate."

So Rory read the book lying in Katherine's bed wearing the cute pin-striped men's pyjamas that Katherine wore to sleep in and a few days later he went down to Leather Lane Market and bought Katherine some stylish designer knock-offs: three skimpy spaghetti-strap T shirts and a tight leather skirt that would show off her lovely little firm bottom.

Rory felt a sudden stab of annoyance at Jenny. "Why wasn't she more like Katherine," he thought to himself, "why didn't she wear sexy clothes and work out at the gym three times a week like the other woman did. Jenny really needed to pull herself together."

"She appreciates Tolstoy's ability in bringing Anna so vividly to life," he told Byron on his second visit "... but ultimately she says she despises her for falling so hysterically in love with such a transparent bastard as Vronsky when her husband is actually a better more moral man. She says she'd never do anything like that, she's got too much self-respect."

They then went on to discuss Katherine's sparkling academic record, the martial arts black belt she possessed and the affair she'd had with Lenny Kravitz. As the two old friends talked on into the evening it dawned on Rory that the awkwardness which had existed since Byron's return from Somalia vanished when they talked about Katherine Walker.

*****

About a week later Byron suddenly asked. "Do you think she's ever had sex with another woman?"

"Who Katherine?"

"Yeah."

"I'll ask her," said Rory, "that's the thing - she's so upfront you can talk easily to her about stuff like that."

"Yes she has," Rory told Byron on his fifth visit. "We had a bottle of wine together late the other night and she told me all about it. She likes men most – her exact words were 'she's got to have a regular supply of dick' – but a couple of times she's had crushes on women and you know... once or twice it's led to, well sex... kissing and fondling and rubbing and stuff... but no sex toys. She thinks that's unnatural."

"Wow," exhaled Byron with a far-away look in his eyes.

"Yeah wow," said Rory. "She told me the thing she noticed when you're like, kissing a woman is how small their mouths are, compared to men's."

"Oh God," said Byron, "I have simply got to meet this woman."

What happens next? Over to you...

The Angel

by Sue Townsend

Sue Townsend is the creator of Britain's best loved and bestselling diarist, Adrian Mole. *Together the Mole diaries have sold over 8 million copies, have been adapted for radio, television, theatre and been translated into 42 languages. Her other novels include* Rebuilding Coventry *(1988),* The Queen and I *(1992) and* Ghost Children *(1998). A collection of her monthly columns for Sainsbury's Magazine was published in 2001 entitled "Public Confessions of a Middle-aged Woman Aged 55 $^3/_4$."*

Sue is currently working on her next novel: Adrian Mole and the Weapons of Mass Destruction.
Sue was born in Leicester in 1946, is married and has four children and seven grandchildren and still lives in Leicester.

MY MOTHER WASN'T GOOD with children, she didn't have the knack. Dogs were her thing. She trained hers to walk on their back legs and she put red satin ribbons in their hair. I used to take her favourite dog, Mitzi, to see her after she was admitted, against her will, to The Laurels nursing home. I would stand on the lawn opposite my mother's room and get Mitzi to wave her paws. My mother would stare out of the window from her bed and then turn her head away and weep. Dogs were not allowed inside, and, for some reason, the old people were not allowed to drink coffee either. My mother eventually died at The Laurels from infected bed sores. I once visited her unexpectedly and found her being spoon fed cold porridge by a schoolboy on work experience. My mother's nightie was open and her breasts were exposed. I complained in writing but the owners wrote back to say that 'my mother's human rights had not been infringed'. I won't allow myself to get old and helpless. I want to die before I'm sixty.

I first met Anthony Adams on my fifty-ninth birthday. He came into the shop to buy a pair of brogues. There had been no birthday cards on my doormat that morning and there were none at work either. I keep my private life to myself. I told Anthony that the brogues came in three colour-ways, black, brown and ox-blood. He screwed his face up as though he were in pain. Some people find it impossible to make a decision. He looked like the managerial type: Tall, authoritative and well dressed. "Black," I said.

It was almost half past five when I went into the storeroom. The other girls had got their coats on and were saying goodnight to each other. We don't have to climb a ladder to reach the stock anymore; it's done electronically, the machinery works, most of the time. But when it seizes up an engineer has to fly in from Germany. Everything is complicated now, even the weather. When I was a girl the winters were cold, you were guaranteed snow and icicles. The summers were always hot. I would walk to school in the morning and the sun would be scorching my back. The important things in our lives were written down and recorded in little books. We had a rent book, an insurance book and a post office book; you could grasp these little books, open them and read them. And you knew where you were. The Gas Board sold gas and the Electricity Board sold electricity, and if you made a telephone call you were answered by a human being. It was a simple life, even in the towns. There were pubs, cinemas, theatres, libraries, swimming baths, an opera house and the circus came twice a year – we didn't know that the animals felt humiliated and that it was cruel of us to laugh at their clumsy antics.

The machinery brought the size eleven brogues down to me. I knelt in front of Anthony and helped him on with his new shoes, he fumbled with the laces. I was anxious to be off, he was pale and sweating and I was alone in the shop with him.

"I don't feel very well." He said.

My heart sank, an image of an ambulance crossed my mind and I thought about the paperwork I would have to fill in and send to head office if he collapsed on me. I asked him if he would like a glass of water and to my annoyance he said he would, so I went into the staff kitchen and ran the tap and waited for the water to turn cold. Meanwhile I watched him on the CCTV, his lips were moving, he could have been praying or singing along to a song he could hear inside his head.

It took a full ten minutes for him to sip the glass dry. He said that something terrible had happened to him recently. To be polite I made sympathetic noises. Before I could stop him he launched into his story.

"I was lying in my bath reading the Sunday papers when I heard the doorbell ring. I live on my own, no wife, no kids, they're long gone – but I thought sod it, whoever it is will go away, but they didn't. That bell rang and rang and rang until I thought I'd go mad. So I got out the bath, wrapped a towel round me and went downstairs. The bell was ringing constantly, like somebody had got their finger stuck. I shouted "For fucks sake!" And snatched the door open. There was a bloke on the doorstep, my height, my build pointing a gun at my head."

He said "Geoff Green?"

I said. "No, I'm Anthony Adams: Geoff lives opposite at number seven."

"And this gunman ran across the road and rang the doorbell. Geoff came round the side of his house; he was carrying a paintbrush with white paint on it. A few words were exchanged then the bloke stood back a bit and fired the gun at Geoff's head. Geoff fell onto his drive; he'd only just had it paved. Some gypsies did it with slabs they nicked off the council – the man with the gun ran down our street, jumped on a motorbike that was parked at the kerb and roared off. I ran across the road in my bare feet holding the towel round my waist. Geoff took a few seconds to die. Bits of his skull and globs of his brain were spattered on the flowers in the tub by the front door."

He looked at me and said "Have you seen a dead body?"

I told him that I'd only seen one, my mother's. He said he'd seen too many.

He sighed. "Poor Geoff." Then he said "I'm responsible for killing him."

I asked him what his name was, and he told me it was Anthony Adams. I said "Do you know why Geoff Green was killed?"

He said "No, and I haven't asked."

I asked him if the police had caught the murderer.

"No, they'll never catch him – he's a professional, a contract killer." He said.

"Why was he killed?" I said.

"I never ask." He said. "But he died happy, he didn't starve to death like some poor buggers do who live only a plane ride from us."

His face softened, I saw what he must have looked like when he was a small child.

I came very close to putting my arms around his neck and pulling his head near to mine. I said "I'd gladly swap places with Geoff Green. I'm tired of living in this world."

He said "You look like a woman who squeezes every last bit of enjoyment out of life."

I told him that appearances are nearly always deceptive. I wanted to tell him that I would like nothing better than to be allowed to fade into darkness, to not exist, be nothing, just to be a speck that disappears into nowhere. But of course I didn't.

He said "I'll take the shoes."

But it was six o'clock and the cash till had turned itself off automatically so I told him he'd have to come back tomorrow.

As I was locking up, setting the alarm, lowering the grill on the door and mobilising the security system he said "Do you know how much he was paid? Two hundred and fifty pounds."

I was amazed.

"Two hundred and fifty pounds." I said. "I've paid more than that for a week in Skegness. I thought contract killing was something only the rich could afford."

"It'll cost you more in London," He said "and for V.I.Ps, but in the provinces, for a nonentity that's the going rate."

He touched my elbow and said "I have a drink in the Angel most nights, would you care to join me?"

I didn't want his pity, I'm fifty-nine, grey and fat, and could have been taken for his mother. So I told him that I had to get back, then I wished him goodnight and watched him as he crossed the road and pushed his way into the bar of the Angel. Before the door closed I heard the sounds of music and laughter.

When I got home I didn't bother with food, I walked straight up the stairs and put myself to bed. I had liked it when he touched my elbow, it's years since I'd been intimate with a man. I was married to my husband for thirteen happy years, then I went up three dress sizes in as many months and he left me for a girl whose thigh he could span with both hands. It wasn't only the weight: It took me too long to get over losing the babies. I forgot how to laugh. My mouth wouldn't smile. I grew tired of people telling me that life must go on.

I don't think I dreamt, the night I met Anthony Adams. I slept really well and I woke up eight hours later, I've not done that for years.

When I got to work he was there waiting at the door.

"I'll pay you for those shoes now." He said.

I was a bit flummoxed, I normally open the door easily enough, but with him watching me I made a few mistakes, the alarm went off and the grill came down but I sorted it out. I asked him to sit down when we got inside while I took my coat off and turned the shop lights on. Then, when the till came on I put his shoes through. He said, "I tell you what, I'll wear the new shoes now."

He sat down and took his shoes off. They didn't look old. He had obviously polished them before he came out. He put his new ones on, did the laces up, went to the mirror and admired them, quite openly admired them. Men don't usually do that, they look through half closed eyes, as if they happened to be passing the mirror.

He handed me his old shoes and said "Can you put these in the bin."

I said, "You can't throw these away, they're hardly worn. Give them to Age Concern, they're only next door."

He laughed and said he would. "It's a few years since I gave to charity."

He seemed reluctant to leave but I had too much to do,

so I said "Thank you Mr. Adams." And he took the hint and left the shop.

At lunchtime I went for a walk around the market and bought myself some sweet apricots and a bunch of jewel coloured anemones. I went into Age Concern and his shoes were there on the rack priced at two pounds fifty. I picked them up and examined them carefully; the leather was so fine that I could see the little bumps where his toes had been. There were stains on the soles that could have been blood. I thought, with a bit of luck I won't be here this time next year. Somebody else will be managing the shoe shop, another person will be living in my house, and yet another driving my car.

Before I went back to work I queued at the hole in the wall and checked the balance in my deposit account. After I retired I wouldn't be able to live in my house and run my car. My pension had been stolen years ago by Robert Maxwell. I withdrew two hundred and fifty pounds.

That night I went through my clothes and threw a lot of stuff away. I found a frock I'd bought but never worn; a cocktaily thing. I put it on and sucked my stomach in. Black sequins glimmered back at me from the mirror on the wardrobe door. I searched through my shoe collection for a pair of black high heels and slid them on. I folded my hair into a French Pleat, made my face up carefully and drove back into town, to the Angel. I'm not a drinker and I didn't know what to ask for at the bar. The barman suggested a snowball;

"They're very popular with the ladies" He said.

I looked around the bar; Anthony Adams was sitting in the corner, alone reading the Daily Telegraph and drinking beer from a pint glass. He was wearing his new shoes. I sucked my stomach in and walked over to him. He folded his paper away and invited me to sit down. I sipped at my drink, "Ugh, it's slimy and disgusting." I said.

"You don't have to finish it." Anthony said, "Nobody's holding a gun to your head."

What happens next? Over to you...

One Size Fits All

by Fay Weldon

Fay Weldon was born in 1931 and moved from New Zealand to England as a teenager. After a spell in advertising (she coined the slogan Go To Work On An Egg), she became one of Britain's most famous feminist writers. She was first published in 1967 and since then has written many novels (including The Life and Loves of A She Devil*), five collections of short stories (the latest – "Nothing to Wear and Nowhere to Hide"), an autobiography (*Auto Da Fay*), as well as many dramas for TV, stage and radio.*

Fay is married, has four sons and lives in Dorset.

THE TROUBLE WAS IT DIDN'T. One size did not fit all. People hoped it would, and talked and acted as if it did, but it just didn't. There were always people left out of the loop and she, Ursula, would always be one of them. Fate had presented her with literal evidence of this painful truth some years back, when she was 28, in the tenth year of her marriage, and in the accessories department of Bergdorf Goodman, a very select store on Fifth Avenue, New York. There had been a particularly lovely belt on sale, soft Italian leather fastened with an elaborate hand-made silver buckle. The label said 'One Size Fits All'. Ursula put the belt around her waist and the ends didn't meet at all, let alone leave any extra trim to be cut away. The label lied.

One size fits all regular people, but I am not regular, I do not belong. This belt is a symbol of both my strength and my discontent. I do not fit in, I never will. I am an outcast, a size 12, in a city where the lean, glossy-haired, well-exercised women who inhabit it think a size 6 is vast.

Then she'd looked at the price tag. $1,735. That was absurd. The buckle might be a work of art but it was still just a belt. She went back to the hotel and told her husband David about it, and he said that American women were a different shape to European women, broad shoulders and wide ribcages but with narrow waists and hips, so you'd expect belts on the whole to be shorter than in Europe, where the women tended to be pear shaped. David was in the fashion business.

"You should have bought it," David said, "If you liked it. They'd have made you one up especially, at that price. We have more than enough money to spend." But she couldn't see the point. Better save the money. One day they might be penniless again.

That must have been how long ago, seventeen, eighteen years ago? Now, aged 44, she sat in a state of terror in the departure lounge of Bristol Airport. She was waiting for a flight to Milan, where she would join David for the fashion shows. She was flying economy – why waste money – and had rashly told the girl at check-in that she suffered from fear of flying, expecting sympathy, and the girl had just given her a look which said "God, you are so pathetic." It was the 'One Size Fits All' syndrome again: if you weren't like everyone else and drew attention to that fact you were despised.

Her fear of flying, she told friends, was totally reasonable.It was not to be afraid which was peculiar. Those machines were heavier than air: you could not trust them to stay aloft. And her experiences of aircraft had not been good. She'd taken her first flight when she was eighteen as an art student, going on a traumatic family holiday to the Canaries. By the end of the two weeks her parents were no longer together, and had flown home separately. After that there had been marriage to David and babies, and no money, and nowhere to fly to anyway, and then when she was 21 her best friend Allie had died in an air crash. If Ursula was reluctant to board an aircraft who could be surprised? For 27 stubborn but satisfactory years she had never gone anywhere by air. And now see what had happened. She had been made anxious, upset, undermined by others, so that the fear of flying to Milan was suddenly less than the fear of what might happen if she didn't. The board which until now had said 'Wait in Lounge' now said 'Delayed 30 mins.' There was a rustle of impatience around her, but Ursula was glad. Thirty minutes more life.

She tried to relax her body, un-tense her neck, remember the skills of her yoga class. She realised she had been holding her breath, which didn't help, and now she tried to breathe regularly and deeply. What had it been like for Allie, when the flight had plunged downwards? She couldn't get that out of her head. Did you scream? Could you breathe? Ursula had taken in Allie's two small children and brought them up as hers and David's own: relatives usually did that but there were none. So excuse her if she didn't choose to fly. 'One-size- fits-all' need not apply. If she saw the check-in girl she might start talking loudly about air crashes. She felt belligerent.

She didn't want to be the one the belt didn't fit. She didn't want to be the reluctant flyer, the one the check-out girl sneers at for a coward and a neurotic. She didn't want to be the one who thought $1,735 was too much to pay for a belt, when there was more than enough money to go round. She wanted to be brave and generous, the kind of person who didn't feel frightened when she saw a banking aircraft against a city sky scape, who didn't save frequent traveller air miles, who wasn't mean with other people's money, who was in fact like other people. "Poor David," people said, and Ursula knew they said it, "having to put up with a wife like her, just because they married you, when he could have had a new 'one-size-fits-all' wife, someone more given to personal adornment, someone fashionable, who loved parties and didn't loathe caterers, who didn't wear an artist's smock and make faces at photographers, and helped her husband on in his career." There were enough women around like that, everyone knew, bright and beautiful and available, ready to wind long arms and legs around any rich, successful man and snap him up.

"All those beautiful women he meets," they'd say, in their 'one-size-fits-all' voices. "The most beautiful women in the world. And still he sticks with her."

"But I don't want you to be like anyone else," said David, if ever Ursula agitated. "I only like you." By 'like' he meant 'love.' She knew that.

A voice regretted that the flight had been delayed. There had been technical trouble with the incoming aircraft. Oh yes, thanks very much. Very reassuring. The thirty minutes was now up to fifty.

They had been married since they were nineteen, and both at art school in Cardiff. He was doing fashion and fabric, she was doing fine art. Now he provided fabrics for all the big fashion houses, was on first name terms with everyone from Donatella to Jean Paul. While David flew about the world growing rich she had four children, two their own and two Allie's, now all grown and gone, and painted portraits in the studio in the garden. She would drop her paint brushes and go by boat and train to be with David when she could, but more and more often she couldn't. Things moved so fast, these days, or perhaps she moved a little more slowly. Her subjects came to her, she didn't have to go to them.

The time they'd been in New York they'd got there in a cruise ship (boats were bad enough – think of the Titanic; size did not guarantee safety – but certainly better than aircraft.) The Paris shows were a doddle these days, thanks to Eurostar – though she had to take tranquilisers for the tunnel part of the journey – and Italy was manageable thanks to the train, but you could forget Hong Kong or Australasia or the new markets opening up in China. David had to go on his own. And he went a lot.

"I think you're out of your mind," her mother would say. "Just face the fear, get over it. It's crippling your life. A man like that, with a bank balance like that could have any woman in the world, and you let him go off on his own!"

"David's not like that," was all she'd say. She wouldn't add 'he loves me,' because her mother would just laugh at her. Men! You could trust them no further than you could throw them. Ursula's mother knew that for a fact and Ursula should know that too. Ursula's father had followed his fancy where it led him and that was mostly into other women's beds, and when Ursula was eighteen and on a family holiday Ursula's mother had finally had enough. Had her daughter forgotten all that?

"David has to go out to work," she never said to her mother, "and he adores the thrill and fantasy and neuroses of the fashion world, but all he really wants to do in the world is lie in bed beside me where it's warm and soft, and I quite like painting pictures but it's the same for me, what we want most in all the world and ever will is each other."

"Tell me another," her mother would only say, so why try and explain. Ursula's mother was a 'one-size-fits-all' person; all men are villains, don't trust the police, don't believe your teachers, life itself is a conspiracy against the living.

"I know a good hypnotist," her mother had said lately. "He specialises in fear of flying. You need to get out there to be with David. He's good looking, he's charming, he's hetero in a gay world and you're a fool and growing older."

Ursula had tried, or gone through the motions of trying. She'd been to counsellors, hypnotists, even been to customer confidence classes run by British Airways and come away more terrified than ever. Seeing the instrument panels had not reassured her one bit. All those winking lights and thousands of little things to go wrong – worse than not knowing, shutting your eyes.

She didn't have to get on the plane. She had her overnight bag with her. All she had to do was go back through security – they let you do that – and get in a taxi and go home to put herself out of her misery. '60 minutes delay', the board now said. She was angry with herself and with her friend Frances, whose fault this mainly was. Frances had frightened her. For the first time in her life Ursula lacked trust; Ursula doubted. She was reduced to checking up on David. It was seedy and horrible and new.

Frances, a fashion journalist, had been dropping hints about Lola Hassenburg, David's assistant, for the last few months. "But she's so pretty," Frances said. "All that red hair and that bosom draping all over his desk. It's silicone, but men don't seem to mind. You've got to get rid of her."

"Look," said Ursula, finally, "David gets to work with all the top models. I am not in competition with them, how could I be? They're more like race horses than human beings, they're a really odd shape, they have spotty backs. There's more to a human being than looks. To him they're just more colleagues. It's the same with Lola. She's a brilliant seamstress and she can read David's mind and he likes her and she's very pretty but she's thick as two planks, has a whiny voice, and he's got nothing to talk to her about outside the workshop."

"It's not talking I'm worrying about," said Frances. "You are the nicest person in the world but I wish you knew how to look after yourself."

And then just before Milan David had called her and said why didn't she fly out to be with him, there would be a lot of old friends turning up and Ursula had said no she couldn't. But it was strange of him to ask, because suggesting his wife flew anywhere was absurd. She'd called the workshop where they were working late and asked to speak to Lola and someone there said Lola had just flown off to Milan, and then "woops, sorry!" She called David and said which old friends, give them her love, and had asked casually if Lola was going to be there and he'd said no. So she said well have a good time, see you back home on Thursday, and had called the airport straight away and found a flight to Milan. And now she sat in the departure lounge, waiting. And her breathing was all wrong again and palms were sweaty with fear, and she was wondering if Lola and David were booked into the same room, and she needed to find out.

The interesting thing about fear of flying was what exactly it was you were frightened of. She did not mind death one bit. She had brought up four children and painted some good portraits and loved a husband and that was enough. She would hate the crashing, falling, fearful bit Allie had been through, of course, but she was getting older, David would marry again – she would see that as a compliment – he might even have more children and spread his genes a little more widely. They were good genes. The world deserved them. It was not death she had ever feared, it was what would happen when she got to her destination. What would happen on the Canary Isles, what would happen to Allie's children when Allie got to where she was fated to go, what would happen if she went places with David. It wasn't the journey she dreaded it was the arriving. She'd told herself she was the kind of person who didn't fly, who had been brought up in a background where there was no money to fly, flying was what other people did, holidays were what other people took, she was the 'one-size-fits-all' person whom the belt didn't fit, but none of that was true.

What she worried about was what would happen if the plane didn't crash, if she didn't die, if she had to live without David because David was with someone else, like Lola Hassenburg, red hair all over the pillow.

What she saw as trust and faith was folly, and her mother tried to tell her so and Frances too and she wouldn't face it. And if she got on this plane NOW she would finally have to. Of course her palms were sweaty. And now the notice board began to change violently and the '90 mins. delay' was running up numbers and changed to Now Boarding and the voice said another aircraft had been flown in from Heathrow and was actually at the gate. And they would soon be on their way. It was a friendly, reassuring voice.

The girl from the check-in desk passed her on the way to the gate, where she would now collect boarding cards, and paused by Ursula and said "You know, you are more likely to die on the car journey from the airport here than on the flight itself. Don't worry." And Ursula got to her feet.

What happens next? Over to you...

The Tunnel

by Shaun Hutson

Shaun Hutson alias 'The Godfather of Gore' made his name as a horror writer with novels like Slugs, Spawn *and* Relics. *His first book,* Slugs, *has now sold more than 500,000 copies. Latterly, he has moved away from horror, penning what he describes as "urban thrillers." Shaun's consuming passion is football. A Liverpool supporter for over 30 years, he never misses a game, home or away. He has appeared on stage with heavy-metal rock band Iron Maiden 13 times.*

Shaun lives with wife, daughter and two pairs of Michelle Pfeiffer's shoes in Buckinghamshire.

THE BLEEDING HAD STOPPED within minutes of the thumb being severed.

Frank Tate dropped it into a small plastic bag then glanced impassively at the digit for a moment. There was a small tattoo on the lower knuckle that looked like a staring eye. Tate had been careful to cut around the base with the knife to ensure that the tattoo remained intact. He didn't want the skin torn too badly. It was the mark on the flesh that would identify the owner and that was important to the men who had hired Tate. They would want to be sure that the possessor of that tattoo was dead. Tate had considered taking them the whole hand but decided only the severed digit was necessary. It would be enough to get him his money.

Sometimes polaroids were sufficient. On other occasions, merely pieces of clothing. Once, a whole head. Tate didn't care. When he was hired to do a job he delivered. Literally. He looked once more at the hacked off thumb, swathed in clear-wrap inside the bag, then slid it into his jacket pocket.

The serrated kitchen knife he'd used for his makeshift surgery lay close to the body. It bore no fingerprints. Neither did the garotte of electrical flex fastened so tightly around the neck of the man who lay at Tate's feet.

It was Tate's favoured method. It was relatively quick and there was usually only a small amount of blood. Sometimes the victim would bite off their own tongue but he could only recall that happening twice. There was the usual voiding of bladder and bowels as death took them. But never more than specks of blood. Occasionally he got some on his gloves but it cleaned off easily enough. And if it didn't then he burned them and bought more. Always the finest leather that fitted his large hands like a second skin. When you were at the top of your profession, as Tate had been for eight years, he saw this kind of thing as a necessity rather than an indulgence. A reward for his prowess in his chosen field.

He took one last look around the room then walked unhurriedly down the stairs and out into the street where he hailed a cab.

As the taxi finally pulled up outside the station, Tate glanced at his watch. The train he wanted to catch left in less than five minutes. He glared at the back of the taxi driver's head, blaming the man for not having made better time through relatively light late night traffic. Tate stuffed a couple of notes into the man's outstretched hand and sprinted off without waiting for change.

As he reached the concourse he looked up at the electronic ARRIVALS and DEPARTURES board, checked the platform number he needed then increased his pace.

He began to think he wouldn't make it in time. He ran as fast as he could, legs churning, feet thundering on the tarmac ramp but, despite the fact that the slope favoured him by inclining down towards the platform, he still had doubts about his ability to reach the train before it pulled away.

Uniformed attendants, resplendent in brightly coloured jackets, waited. No members of the public were to be seen. Those who had come to say goodbye to travellers had now wandered off. Any tearful farewells had been concluded.

Tate ran on. Outside the blackness of the night was punctuated by street lights, the glow from shop signs and the headlamps of various passing vehicles but inside the terminus itself only the dull glow of bulbs high in the roof gave off any illumination.

Tate's breath rasped in his throat, his heart hammered hard against his ribs. His chest ached from the effort of sucking breath into lungs that were already burning and his mouth felt as if someone had filled it with chalk.

He saw the last remaining staff member on the platform turn to the nearest train door and clamber through it. The figure called something to him but he couldn't make out the words.

His grasping fingers finally closed over the cold metal of the handle and he twisted it, hauling himself inside. Slamming the door behind him, almost overbalancing.

Made it.

He felt the train lurch slightly as it began to move away, steadily building up speed. For a moment or two he stood with his hands on his hips, breathing heavily. Then he wiped perspiration from his forehead with the back of one hand, patted the jacket pocket where the severed thumb nestled and walked through into the first carriage.

As he made his way slowly up the aisle he counted three other occupants of the First Class compartment. A woman in her thirties was seated at one of the larger tables, tapping away at a laptop. Tate guessed she was a year or two younger than him. Further up from her, a balding man in a white shirt was reclining in his seat, listening to music on a portable CD player, his fingers tapping gently on the arm of his chair. The third traveller was younger. Mid-twenties. He was looking at a magazine and cast a cursory glance in Tate's direction before returning to his reading matter.

Tate sat down in one of the single seats and let out a deep sigh somewhere between relief and satisfaction. He settled into his seat, peering out into the blackness of the night, aware that the train was now increasing its speed as it left the station further behind. He could see the lights of houses on both sides of the tracks. To his right, vehicles moved along a stretch of road then disappeared out of sight. Tate stretched, the muscles of his legs aching from the sprint he'd been forced to make. A slight smile played on his lips and he caught sight of his reflection in the window. All he had to do now was sit there and let the train carry him on through the night.

He would make the delivery the following morning. And when the merchandise was approved he would pick up his money and leave. Until the next job.

He could hear the clicking of keys as the woman worked on her laptop and, more than once, he heard her voice as she answered a call on her mobile phone.

Tate lounged there a moment listening to the sound of the train and gazing absently out of the windows into the night.

He was startled from his aimless peering by the hiss of the hydraulic door leading into the carriage. A uniformed woman carrying two metal jugs walked in and stopped at each of the occupants of the compartment to ask if they wanted tea or coffee.

Tate hauled himself upright in his seat as she drew closer and he watched as she poured coffee into his cup. He thanked her then stirred the steaming beverage as she made her way back up the compartment and disappeared from view again.

Despite the coffee, he felt tired. His frantic rush to reach the train coupled with the comforting warmth inside the carriage made him feel pleasantly drowsy and he reclined his seat slightly, welcoming the onset of sleep.

Ahead of him, the tapping of the laptop keyboard had ceased momentarily as the woman sipped her own hot drink. Tate caught her eye and was pleasantly surprised when she smiled back at him. He returned the gesture and settled lower in his seat, his head lolling to one side, his eyes turned towards the darkness beyond the well-lit interior of the carriage. The night looked like a black towel thrown over the landscape. Tate couldn't even see street lights anymore. Or headlamps. He frowned slightly as he realized that they hadn't passed through a station yet.

Had they?

He looked at his watch. The train had been travelling at top speed for more than twenty minutes now. And yet, beyond the carriage windows, there were no lights of any kind. It was as if they were in a tunnel. But there was none of the familiar amplified noise that came with the passage of one of those subterranean shafts. In fact, it seemed almost unduly quiet within the compartment.

Tate looked away from the window in the direction of the woman at the laptop.

There was only empty space where she'd been sitting.

She must, he reasoned, have gone to the toilet or perhaps to the buffet car further up the train. He leaned to one side and looked up the aisle.

No fingers drumming on the arm of the chair in time to music. The man in the white shirt was missing too.

Tate stood up, trying to catch sight of the younger man at the far end of the carriage.

Three magazines and a mobile phone lay on the table but, of the younger passenger, there was no sign.

Tate sat down again and took to gazing back out of the window. His brow, already creased, acquired several more furrows as he noticed that there still seemed to be no respite from the tenebrous gloom outside. No sign of a light anywhere. If the train was indeed passing through a tunnel then it was one of quite astonishing length, thought Tate.

The ringing of a mobile phone interrupted his musings.

It took him a second to realize that it was the phone on the table near the carriage door. He rose from his seat again, as if expecting that the younger passenger who'd left the phone there would magically re-appear to answer it.

Tate stepped out into the aisle, the tune played by the musical ringtone now beginning to irritate him a little. Wondering where the phone's owner had got to, Tate began striding up the aisle. He passed the table where the woman with the laptop had been sitting. As he drew level he looked at the upturned screen. There were just four words on it;

Terribilis est locus iste

Tate looked more closely at the screen, the irritating phone still ringing in his ears.

He wasn't a stupid man but his knowledge of latin was certainly sparse. Tate glanced at the words once again then moved on up the aisle towards the ringing phone. He peered through into the next compartment, wondering if he might see the young man making his way back to his seat. There was no sign of him. In fact, as Tate stood beside the table, he could see no sign of movement at all in the carriage beyond.

He took a step towards the door which opened automatically. It was cold in the area between the carriages. One of the windows was slightly open and a chill breeze was whipping in. Tate swiftly crossed to the window and shut it. The door of the toilet closest to him was ajar. He placed two fingers tentatively on it and pushed, watching as it swung open to reveal an empty cubicle. He moved across towards the door of the next compartment, pausing a moment to tap lightly on the door of the other lavatory. The sign showed that it was vacant so Tate tapped once again and pushed it. The other toilet was also empty.

He continued into the next carriage, still able to hear the mobile from behind him. He stalked up the aisle, looking to his left and right.

At the first table there was a half empty cup of coffee, steam still rising from it. A little further up he found an overnight bag propped on a table, unzipped to reveal clothes inside. Beside it there was an open newspaper and another cup of coffee, also still steaming. At one of the larger tables he found a half eaten bar of chocolate and another newspaper. There was a biro lying on it, a crossword partially completed. There was a miniature bottle of wine, most of which had been decanted into the glass that rattled gently on the table. There was lipstick on the rim.

Tate saw a slim leather bound book lying next to the wine glass. It had a pen jammed between the pages to keep it open at this chosen place and Tate realized that it was a diary. He reached for it and picked it up, the pen dropping to the floor.

Written across the two pages were four now familiar words;

Terribilis est locus iste

He threw the diary down and continued on up the aisle towards the door of the carriage. He moved through it, seeing more cups full of steaming tea or coffee. Other tables littered with crumbs of food or wrappers. He saw some half eaten sandwiches at one table. A can of fizzy drink standing next to a glass in which ice was melting.

Another two carriages and he would reach the buffet car. Then perhaps he could find some answers.

There was no one in the two compartments leading to the buffet car either but Tate did pause in one of them to inspect the screen of another laptop and the words that flickered upon it.

Terribilis est locus iste

His initial feelings of mild bewilderment had given way rapidly to irritation and now to full blown annoyance.

Where the hell was everyone? Granted he didn't expect a night train to be full to the rafters with passengers, especially not in First Class but this was ridiculous. Why had they left their belongings at their tables? Why the half drunk beverages? Why the abandoned hot drinks? He knew there must be a good reason for it but, as he strode towards the buffet car, he was damned if he could think what that reason might be.

Even in his anger he had sufficient presence of mind to look up at the sign on the end wall of the compartment that proclaimed; TOILET ENGAGED. It glowed with a dull, sickly yellow light but, to Tate, it shone like a golden nugget in a dung heap. If the toilet was engaged there was someone inside. Simple logic. He would wait for the occupant to emerge then ask them a few questions, find out what the hell was going on.

He stood, arms folded, waiting. Five minutes passed. Tate moved closer to the door, listening for any sounds from inside. After another five minutes of silence and stillness elapsed, Tate stepped close to the door and banged hard on it.

Whether the lock was faulty or because of the force of his blows, the door cracked open a fraction.

Tate pushed it.

As it swung open to reveal the cubicle, Tate looked in. He'd been prepared to say something, to speak. To enquire of the occupant if they'd seen anyone else moving about on the train.

The cubicle was empty.

But what Tate saw froze the breath in his lungs.

What happens next? Over to you...

A Woman's Right to Shoes

by Marian Keyes

Marian Keyes was born in Limerick in 1963. Since she was first published in 1995, she has become one of the biggest selling Irish writers of all time. Her seven novels, Watermelon, Lucy Sullivan is Getting Married, Rachel's Holiday, Last Chance Saloon, Sushi for Beginners, Angels *and* The Other Side of the Story *have become international bestsellers, published in twenty-nine languages, selling nine million copies along with three of them becoming movies for TV and general release.*

Marian includes among her hobbies, reading, movies, shoes, handbags and M&Ms, and now lives in Dún Laoghaire with her husband Tony.

THIN MORNING LIGHT, grey pavement, counting forty-eight seconds from the front door to the end of my road. Turn onto bigger road and start again, counting seventy-eight seconds before the traffic lights. Across the road in thirteen, then counting twenty-nine to the shops.

I've only started this counting lark lately – just in the last few weeks. But now I do it all the time, I count everything. It's very handy, it stops me from going mad.

As I got nearer the pub, I wondered if my silver sandal would still be outside. Probably. Because who would want it? Mind you, there was no accounting for pissed people. They took big orange traffic cones home, why not a single, silver sandal?

Nearer I got and nearer; there was something there alright and it was the right size for a shoe. But already I knew it wasn't mine. Alerted by some instinct, already I knew something strange was happening. And sure enough, once I was close enough, I saw that my sandal was gone – and, as if by alchemy, shimmering in its place was a different shoe, a man's shoe. It was astonishingly beautiful: a classic brogue shape, but in an intense purple leather. It sat on the grey pavement, looking almost like it was floating and it seemed to throb, as if it was the only thing of colour in a black and white world. Slightly mesmerised, I picked it up and turned it over. There were no scuffs on the sole, like it had never been worn. Butter-soft, biscuit-coloured leather lined the insides and it made my aching eyes feel better just to look at it.

Should I bring it to the police station? It looked important enough. But it was a shoe, a single shoe. Lost by a man who'd had one alcopop too many last night. I'd be cautioned for wasting police time.

Perhaps I should put up a sign saying it had been found – if it was a puppy or a kitten people would and shoes were beloved also. Next door to the pub was the newsagents with its noticeboard of ads. I could post something there: 'Found: One magical shoe.' Then I remembered the last time I'd placed an ad there about shoes. Look at where that had landed me.

But this shoe was too beautiful to abandon. Quickly I gathered it up, wrapped it in my scarf, put it in my bag and hurried to work.

The previous night.

Yes, perhaps wearing a single high, silver sandal mid-November smacked a little of histrionics. But it was necessary for people to know I was making a statement, a protest, even.

As I had walked to the pub I'd plumped for practicality and worn an old pair of trainers – pre-Hayley trainers that for some reason I had kept, even though I had thought those days were long gone – but just before I entered into the bright, convivial warmth, I took them off and replaced them with a single spindly sandal on my right foot. On my left foot – the shoe-free one – my tights had a hole in the toe. I regarded it steadily. So be it. I couldn't falter now.

Listing to one side, I stood just inside the door – were they here? Not yet. This was good, I could settle myself for maximum impact. There were many sofas – this was a lady-friendly pub – but I required elevation and visibility. I hopalonged to the bar and climbed up onto a stool, then I rotated so that I was facing into the room. You couldn't have missed me or – more importantly – my uneven feet, one shod, one bare.

My eyes were doing that constantly-scudding-swimming-fish thing that very dislocated people do and I counted between events (people coming in, people lighting cigarettes, people gently moving a strand of their girlfriend's hair out of her eyes etc; I started back at zero each new time.) In between the counting, I drank steadily. The plan had been to stick to mineral water, but somehow, between the ongoing, world-dislocating shock and my proximity to strong drink, that fell apart. All evening, I sat, my back rigid with righteousness, waiting for them to appear, but they didn't. This was very annoying. How else could I shame them?

Nick, the barman, though clearly a little bit alarmed by my behaviour, was kind. Unlike Naomi, a mutual friend of mine and Steven's who said, "Alice, please put some proper shoes on, this whole thing, it's just so undignified."

Undignified? Me? I was dignity personified, as much as anyone can be in one sandal and one betighted foot in mid-November. In an attempt to defuse me, Naomi tried subsuming me into her group of sofa-based friends, but I refused to abandon my post.

Around eleven o'clock, I gave up; they weren't coming. I hadn't known for sure they would, the real world isn't like Coronation Street. But they had been sighted there together. Which was very tactless, considering Steven and I used to go there. Not every night, maybe only once or twice a week and as much for food as for drink. (Salmon fishcakes, pacific-rim salads, mocha bread-and-butter pudding, etc. Like I said, a lady-friendly pub.)

As I left, I see-sawed across the pub – now quite crowded, which was unfortunate because my great shoe imbalance was not as instantly visible as I would have wished. Indeed, I feared that several people simply dismissed my side-to-side swaying as the result of inebriation. I was aware of general nudgage as I limped past. I even heard someone say, "So she's pissed, so what? After what's happened, who'd blame her?"

Only when I got through the doors and out into the street did I retrieve my trainers from my bag and take the sandal off. I was going to put the sandal back into the bag, and then I thought, But why bother? What use is it to me now?

So I left it. Exactly mid-way across the two doors (well, as mid-way as I could manage after an evening of grim, heavy drinking.)

I nursed a vague plan that I might do the same the next night with a different shoe. And every night thereafter, until all thirty-one of my shoes were gone. Just over a month, it would take.

How I met Hayley.

Most people are unbalanced. Or asymmetrical, as it's more commonly called; my problem area is my feet: my right foot is a size four and my left a size five. I used to get round the problem by buying shoes in a size five and employing insoles, but it wasn't always a great solution, especially if the objects of my desire were sling-backs or open-toed, minxy stuff.

However, one day I was visited with a brilliant, life-changing idea: if I had a size-four right foot and a size-five left foot, could there be someone in the metropolis I lived in who had a size five right-foot and a size four left-foot. My pedi mirror image. If we could only find each other, we could buy two identical pairs, one in size four, one in size five – and divvy them up according to our needs.

I considered advertising in Time Out or a national newspaper, but in the end I placed an ad on the noticeboard in the local newsagent – and got a reply! A local girl, she lived less than ten minutes walk from me and Steven.

I was wild with excitement before I met her, charmed by the idea of symbiosis, and the thought that this woman would complete me.

I am quite freakishly short and therefore fond of high heelage. (Sometimes when I step out of my four-inch heels, people look around in confusion and ask, "Where's she gone?" and I am obliged to call out, "I'm down here.") Hayley, by contrast, was tall and slender. I feared she would spurn high-heelage and embrace flattage, and unfortunately, most of the time, she did. Right from the start it was a battle of wills and our shared asymmetry didn't kick-start a friendship. From time to time we bumped into each other locally, but we only ever arranged to meet on a 'Need to Buy' basis. Which we did for over two years: in March, when the fresh sandals crop hit the shops and September, when the new boots arrived. There were also occasional unscheduled events – the need for glittery Christmas party shoes or just a random spotting of a beautiful pair, which it would have been criminal to pass up.

Sometimes Hayley was game and agreed to the purchase of sky-scraper heels, which made me happy. Even at the best of times, though, it was never as much fun as I'd expected.

In fact, it was slightly uneasy. But I pretended it wasn't. We were girls! We were shopping for shoes! We had a special bond!

The bottom line was that Hayley was horrible. An important life lesson for me, and one I'd learnt too late – just because someone loves shoes doesn't necessarily mean she's a good person.

When Steven told me he was leaving me for her, the shock plunged me into a grey-tinged nightmare. It was then that I began counting. I even found myself doing it in my dreams, because as soon as I stopped, the panic rose steadily until it threatened to choke me.

There was worse to come. Two days later I came home from work to find that all my size-five shoes had been stolen. Hayley had taken them. I was left with thirty-one single right-foot shoes. The only complete pairs I had left were the boots I stood up in and a manky pair of ancient trainers.

Popular psychology has it that when a person undergoes a trauma – a mugging or perhaps an abandonment – they often respond by thinking they're worthless. As it happened, I hadn't got around to it yet. But Hayley had – even though the trauma was mine. In her eyes, I had become utterly insignificant; after helping herself to my husband, she felt she could take anything else she wanted.

Apparently, she had decided that actually, her feet were suddenly the same size. After a lifetime of one size four and one size five, both her feet were now a size five. An unbelievable turnabout? Well, why not? Was it any more incredible than Steven's defection, after he'd once promised that he'd always love, so much so that he'd married me. (I'd had the shoes – white satin pumps – made specially; for once both my feet were perfectly shod.)

I rang them to ask for my shoes back. Hayley told me to stop harassing them. I said I just wanted the return of my shoes. Hayley said they'd get a barring order.

Deflated as I was, I knew I was in the right. But all that remained to me was the moral high-ground. I decided I would wear a succession of single shoes to the local pub in the hope of shaming them publicly.

*****

That evening, after work, when I emerged from the underground, I was expecting to see photocopied flyers stuck to the lamp-posts. Big bold type asking, Have You Seen This Shoe? Then a blurry photocopy – or an artist's impression even – of the magical purple shoe. 'Last seen on my foot on the 17th of November. Reward offered.'

But there was nothing. Didn't anyone care?

I would have cooked dinner, except I didn't bother eating anymore. I counted my way through three soaps until it was time to go to the pub. Tonight I chose a brown suede boot. Then I wrapped the magic shoe in a soft old pashmina – I was glad to get some use from it, it had cost a fortune and four seconds after I'd bought it, it had plummeted out of fashion.

Nick's face fell as I hopalonged through the pub to the same stool I'd sat on the previous night. I was an embarrassment. Well, tough. I unwrapped the purple shoe, like I was revealing a valuable artefact, and asked if he had any idea who it might belong to. No, he said, but he agreed that it was a magnificent-looking shoe and he was very taken with the Cinderella overtones. "You're like Prince Charming. When you find the bloke who owns the shoe, maybe you'll fall in love."

I looked at him scornfully. "This is no fairy-story. And why," I wanted to know, "do men always think that a new man is the solution to women's problems."

"Sorry," he said quietly, taking the shoe and placing it in a position of high visibility behind the bar. There it remained for the entire evening, but no-one claimed it.

I counted my way through every man who came in, my eyes going straight to their feet, as I sought that special man in one shimmering purple shoe and one besocked foot. But nothing.

Nor was there any sign of Steven and Hayley. When I was leaving, I left my brown boot in the street. Then I went home and slept with the purple shoe on my pillow. It wasn't the first time I'd slept with a shoe, but it had never been someone else's before. It seemed to glow in the dark, filling the room with a benign violet light.

The next morning, on my way to work, I wondered if my abandoned boot would be replaced by another purple shoe, I'd half-expected it to be like the elves and the shoemakers – a new shoe every day. But this time there was nothing except an empty cigarette box and that didn't count.

Days passed and I brought the purple shoe everywhere. I felt edgy (ok, edgier) without it and sometimes, when even the counting wasn't working, I took it out of my bag and touched it to my face and, amazingly, it calmed me down. One night I had a dreadful scare when I couldn't find it in my bag to put on my pillow. I was deeply unsettled without it. But when I woke in the morning, it was on my bedroom carpet, twinkling at me as it always did, like a puppy happy to see me. Now, how had that happened? Magic? Or simple muddlement brought about by a surfeit of alcohol? I didn't care, I was massively relieved and hugged the shoe to me.

Mind you, now and then I caught a glimpse of my behaviour, as seen from the outside, and wondered about it. But I'd had my husband stolen and all my left-foot shoes stolen. If I was a little unhinged, who could blame me?

Every night I went to the pub, sat on a stool, and watched for one-shoed men. Every night I wore one shoe and left it behind when I went home. Although I had left nine shoes on nine different nights there had been no sightings of Hayley and Steven.

One night I arrived at the pub to find Nick bubbling over with excitement. "I have your Cinderella," he hissed. "He was here the night before you found the shoe. And he's the kind of bloke who'd have a cool shoe like that." He jerked his head discreetly. "It's him over there."

I looked and immediately I knew this wasn't our man. This one was too good-looking. Wasn't it traditional to make approaches to the ugly sisters first?

However, we went through the motions and actually, he wasn't even nice about it. He seemed baffled when I withdrew the purple shoe from my bag, then he looked at my feet, at the shiny black stiletto on one foot and the big toe poking through the hole in the tights on the other. (Yes, all my tights had developed holes.) Fear scooted across his face; he suspected he was being set-up, that he was the subject of a big, shoe-based leg-pull and that the whole pub was in on it. "That's not my shoe." He dropped eye-contact, then moved away as fast as anyone can in Oliver Sweeney chelsea boots. Seconds later, he left.

Nick and I exchanged a look. "It was worth a try," I said, then Nick went back to polishing glasses and I resumed counting and drinking.

"Give me another look at it," Nick asked later. "Remind me of the brand name again."

I unfolded the pashmina and purpleness blazed

around the bar-counter. Nick and I shared another meaningful look.

I knew what he was thinking: normal non-magical shoes don't behave that way.

The brand name was picked out in gold-leaf on the leather insole. Merlotti.

"I'll look it up on the internet," Nick said.

"No point," I said. I'd already googled the brand and got nothing...

Suddenly a voice behind me cut into our conversation. "Excuse me," it said, "But that's my shoe!"

What happens next? Over to you...

Love or Money

by Ed McBain

Ed McBain is one of the most enduring and illustrious names in crime fiction. His bestselling previous titles include Ice, Candyland, Money Money Money, Fat Ollie's Book *and* The Frumious Bandersnatch. *Ed has also written a number of screenplays, most notably Alfred Hitchcock's* The Birds. *In 1998, he was the first non-British author to be awarded the Crime Writers' Association/Cartier Diamond Dagger Award. He also holds the Mystery Writers of America's coveted Grand Master Award and the Sherlock Award for Best International Detective.*

Ed McBain has been writing successful crime fiction for over 50 years and lives in the United States.

THE RESTAURANT WAS FREQUENTED by the city's literati, a place neither Carella nor Meyer could afford on their annual salaries as Detectives/Second Grade. They were here only because the Medical Examiner had isolated the cause of Helen McReady's death as arsenic poisoning, and they wanted to know if there was any rat poison on the premises.

"We don't have rats in this restaurant," Martha Bailey told them. "Except for the two legged variety."

The food here was reputed to be atrocious, but you'd never have guessed that from the crowds the place attracted or the girth of its eponymous owner, who reportedly ate her own fare and who had to weigh at least as much as a baby elephant. Some forty years old and wearing what the hippies used to call a granny gown, patterned in paisley, Martha stood in stout blonde defiance, her hands on her hips, challenging the detectives to find either rats or rat poisons in her pristine kitchen.

"Who do you mean by two-legged rats?" Meyer asked.

Bald and burly with china-blue eyes and the patience of a safe-cracker, Meyer stood beside Carella in the midst of all these glistening pots and pans and spoons and ladles and mixing bowls. Both men were wearing light-weight, light-colored suits in defense against the torrid August weather. Carella had the casual bearing of an athlete. Head slightly cocked, brown eyes slanting a bit downward to give him a somewhat oriental appearance. He seemed intensely interested in just how Martha Bailey would answer his partner's question about two-legged rats.

"Writers," she said.

"I thought writers liked this place," Carella said.

"Doesn't mean I like writers, "Martha said.

Talk about biting the hand, Carella thought.

"Did Helen McReady come here often?" he asked.

"Only with Harold."

"Harold?"

"Ames. Her editor at the paper. I tried to discourage it but he's a regular. Writers get nervous when a critic's on the premises."

"So how come she chose this place for her birthday party?"

"She didn't," Martha said. "Harold made the booking. He comes here a lot. Sometimes alone with her. They were… ah, very close, shall we say."

An arched eyebrow.

"Meaning?" Carella said.

"Listen, speak no ill of the dead, am I right? The lady was happily married. Enough said."

Meyer and Carella exchanged a glance.

"Made the booking for what time?" Meyer asked.

"Eight."

"What time did they leave?"

"Must have been ten, ten thirty. And by the way she was perfectly fine when they left."

"Where were they sitting?"

"Harold's usual table. Come, I'll show you," she said and led them out of her spotless kitchen.

Martha had decorated the dining room the way she thought an old colonial tavern might have looked. Or should have looked. Heavy wooden beams from which long stemmed, white clay pipes were hanging. Pewter tankards lined up on shelves behind the bar. High-backed wooden booths with cushion seats. Candles in sconces on all the walls. Lanterns hanging all over the place. Carella expected George Washington to ride in on a white horse.

"This is where Harold likes to sit," she said, and showed them one of the larger round tables. "I save it for him whenever he books."

"So who was at this party?" Carella asked.

"Well, Harold and Mrs McReady, of course, and her

husband, go figure." Another arching of the eyebrow. "And her little actress friend. Just the four of them. Cosy"

"Which little actress friend would that be?" Meyer asked.

"Well, actress," Martha said, and pulled a face. "She's a chorus girl actually. Playing in a little musical up the street. All dimples and long legs."

"What's her name? Would you know?"

"Sure. Cyndie Carr. With a 'y' and an 'i,e'. The Cyndie."

"Who do you think poisoned Mrs McReady?" Carella asked.

"Nobody got poisoned in my restaurant," Martha said flatly.

*****

"At first I thought it was just something she'd eaten," George McReady said. "I was feeling fine, but I'd ordered a steak, and she had the trout. So I thought maybe the fish was tainted. Unless…"

They were sitting just outside the funeral home's viewing room, where his wife's corpse was displayed in an open coffin. McReady seemed truly grief-stricken. A thin, almost gaunt man in his early sixties, they supposed. He sat twisting his gnarled hands, unable to stop the tears that streamed down his face.

"Chills aren't a symptom are they?" he asked. "She was feeling a little chilly earlier. In the restaurant. But that must have been the air-conditioning don't you think? She was sitting right under one of the vents, even I felt a bit chilly and I was sitting on the other side of the table. Cyndie offered her a shawl. She was still chilly, but I don't think that was the poison. I don't think chills are a symptom are they?"

"When did you suspect she might have been poisoned, Mr McReady?"

"Well, when she began vomiting. That was when I became truly alarmed. What she brought up had the consistency of rice water, so I knew at once that something…"

"When was this, Mr McReady?"

"Shortly after we got home. Well, we were already in bed. Midnight? Around then? She'd been complaining of a burning pain in her stomach and a sore throat. But then she began vomiting and her skin got clammy, so I rushed her to the hospital. By then her face was turning bl…"

He broke into fresh sobs and buried his own face in his hands.

"Were all four of you drinking the same thing?" Carella asked.

"What?"

"The wine. The beer. Whatever."

"Oh. I don't know what the others were drinking. Helen had a martini before dinner and white wine with the fish. Yes, that's right, I remember now. Harold ordered a bottle of Merlot for himself and me... we were both eating steak... and a Chardonnay for Helen and Cyndie. She was eating veal, I think. Cyndie."

"Who poured the wine?" Meyer asked.

"The waiter, I think. Why?"

Anger suddenly blazed in his eyes like an open fire in the midst of quenching sobs.

"Never mind the waiter," he said. "It wasn't any damn waiter who poisoned her."

They knew when to shut up and listen.

"Both of them had motives," he said bitterly. "They were both furious with Helen."

"Why was that Mr McReady?"

"Simple jealousy! I knew about Harold all along, of course, it had been going on between them for a long time. You make adjustments. A marriage is making adjustments, isn't it? But this was something new. Another woman? A cheap little lesbian whore? Helen never seemed... well... that way."

They kept listening.

"When I learnt that Harold had invited Cyndie to the party, I begged him to phone her again, tell her it was called off, tell her anything. Didn't he know they were lovers?"

McReady shook his head.

His tears had stopped.

His hands were tightly clenched.

They waited for something more.

Patience, Meyer was thinking.

"The chills couldn't have been a symptom." McReady said, as if trying to convince himself, nodding, remembering. "Because once she moved from under that vent, she was alright again. Changed seats, and was cheerful, laughing, drinking. Everything still boy-girl-boy-girl, well, sure," he said, "They were both there to celebrate her birthday, right? Both her little darlings," he said bitterly, and began sobbing again.

*****

They found Cyndie Carr in a second-floor exercise room just off the Stem, close to the theatre district and her apartment. She did not look like she needed any fitness routines. Some five-feet nine inches tall, wearing black tights and a sweat-stained black tank top that scooped low over somewhat exuberant breasts, she came off a treadmill with her hand extended, long blonde hair stringy and damp, dimpled smile on her face, blue eyes flashing.

"Hi," she said, "Whussup?"

Just as if someone hadn't been killed the night before.

They always wondered about the ones who pretended murder was merely par for the course. In their experience, these were the ones who were either plain stupid or were hiding something. Cyndie Carr didn't appear to be stupid, but neither could they imagine what she might be hiding. Unless she was the one who'd poisoned Helen McReady .

"Glad you could make time for us," Carella said.

"Just barely," Cyndie said, sighing, straddling one of the press benches. "I've got to be back at rehearsal by two," she said, and glanced up at the clock on the gymnasium wall. Everywhere around them, good-looking men and women were prancing and lifting and flexing and grimacing. Made Meyer want to go on a diet. Carella too.

"So tell us about last night," he said.

"You know… do I need a lawyer here or anything?" Cyndie asked.

"Why would you think that, Miss Carr?"

"Hey," she said.

They waited.

"Helen was poisoned, duh?" she said, and twirled a forefinger in her dimpled cheek.

"These are just routine questions," they assured her.

"I'll bet," she said.

"How'd you happen to get invited to this party?" Carella asked.

"Helen invited me. Well, actually it was Harold who called me. It was his party, after all. But Helen's the one who suggested it." She hesitated. "We're friends," she said. "Were."

"How long had you known her?"

"She came back after a show I was doing a few months ago. Little musical based on Jane Austen's Sense and Sensibility. Folded in a week, but Helen liked it. Well, love or money, you know how she felt about that. So we started talking…"

"Where was this, Miss Carr?" Carella asked.

"I just told you. Backstage. My dressing…"

"Oh. When you said she came back, I thought you meant she returned…"

"No, I meant backstage. To tell me how much she'd enjoyed the show. And we got to talking, and one thing led to another, and we met for lunch the next day, and became friends. Which is why I was at the party. Because Helen asked Harold to invite me. But, you know…"

They waited.

"Never mind," she said.

"No, what, Miss Carr?"

"I think if we're gonna talk some more here, I'd better call a lawyer. Because, I have to tell you, this doesn't sound at all routine, guys, and I sure as hell don't want to be accused of murdering my best friend in the entire world. Got it?" she said, her face beginning to crumble.

"Got it," Carella said. "Thanks for your time."

"Sure," she said, and turned away to hide the sudden tears in her eyes.

*****

"There are only two things worth writing about," Harold Ames was telling them. "Love or money."

He was in his early fifties, they guessed, lean and green-eyed, with brown hair and a neatly trimmed beard, sitting in slatted sunshine behind a vast desk in his air-conditioned corner-window office. It was now two in the afternoon, and they were here at the newspaper not to listen to literary suppositions, but to learn about that dinner party last night.

"Do you know who said that? Ames asked.

"No, who said it?"

"Helen herself. Well, Jane Austen said it long before Helen did, but she was fond of repeating it. Those words were her credo, in fact and many writers disliked her for it."

"Anyone in particular?" Meyer asked. "These writers who disliked her?"

"Thousands," Ames said. "You can't be the book reviewer for the most influential newspaper in the country, and not expect to make enemies."

Enemies, Carella thought.

A much stronger word than 'disliked'.

"Tell us about the party last night," he said.

"Are we all suspects here?" Ames asked. He seemed amused by the thought.

"No, my partner and I aren't," Carella said.

"I meant the three of us."

"Are any of you writers?"

"Oh, I see, " Ames said.

They waited to see what he had seen.

"You think... because I said writers disliked her, that perhaps a writer poisoned her. Is that it?"

They said nothing.

"There were hundreds of writers in Martha Bailey's last night," Ames said.

Narrows the field a bit, Carella thought.

"Were any if them at your table?" he asked.

"Writers were stopping at the table all night long, sucking up to Helen."

"How do you mean?" Meyer asked.

"Glad-handling her, all smiles, hello, Helen, how have you been? Paying their respects, you know. Looking for that good review on the next book."

"You're saying..."

"I'm saying there were wine glasses sitting right there

in the open. I don't know what the lethal dose of arsenic is…"

"Three grains," Carella said.

"Which is about what? A teaspoon?"

"Much less than that. A pinch, actually. However much she ingested it was enough to kill her in four hours."

"What I'm saying is any one of those ass-kissers could have leaned over the table and dropped it in her glass."

And if pigs had wings, they would fly, Carella thought.

"What was your relationship with Helen McReady?" he asked flat out.

"I'm editor of the book page. That was our relationship. Editor to reviewer."

"That why you dined alone together so often?"

"I didn't realize we dined alone together all that often. But yes. We had many things to discuss."

"Love?" Meyer asked. "Or money?"

"Books," Ames said.

"When did you learn that she was having an affair with Cyndie Carr?"

"Is that a fact?"

"George McReady seems to think so."

"Jealous husband," Ames said, and shrugged.

"How about jealous lover?"

"Mr. McReady says he phoned to ask you to dis-invite Cyndie to the party. Is that true?"

"I couldn't very well do that, now could I? I invited her because Helen asked me to."

"She give you any reason for that?"

"She didn't have to. It was her birthday, after all. But, yes, they were friends."

"Intimate friends, according to McReady."

"Well, as I said, a jealous…"

"Didn't he tell you that Cyndie and his wife were lovers?"

"How'd you feel about that, Mr. Ames?"

"Didn't he specifically say…?"

"Gentlemen," Ames said, and spread his hands on the air. "Please. This isn't a police station, and I'm not under arrest here."

"You ordered the wine last night, isn't that right?"

"Yes."

Curtly now. Lips tightly compressed. Angry frown on his face.

"The red for you and McReady, the white for Cyndie and Helen."

"If you say so."

"Well, they did drink wine from the same bottle didn't they? Cyndie and Helen?"

"I wasn't checking to see who drank what. In fact, I wasn't even at the table all the time."

"Oh? Where were you?"

"I recall going to the men's room at one point."

"Was this after you dropped the arsenic in Helen's glass?"

Ames said nothing.

"Because if the poison wasn't in the bottle itself..."

"... it had to've been dropped in her glass."

"Isn't that so Mr Ames?"

Still nothing.

"Did you put that poison in her glass, Mr Ames?"

"The waiter poured the wine," he said flatly, ticking off the points like a schoolmaster. "Red for George and me, white for the ladies. Helen was complaining about the air conditioning. I excused myself to go to the gents'. She seemed her usual cheerful self by the time I came back to the table. George proposed a toast, and we all drank. If someone poisoned her wine while I was gone..."

Ames shrugged.

"Is that it, gentlemen?" he asked. "Because I have work to do, you see."

What happens next? Over to you...

Entry Details

Please ensure that you have read, and agreed to the following rules and entrant's agreement. If you enter the competition we will take it that you have read, and agree to abide by, these rules.

The story must be:

- The ending to one of the eight short stories which have been written for End of Story.

- Your own work, original and unpublished.

- Maximum of 1,200 words in length, and typed legibly, with double spacing, on single sides of A4. Submissions exceeding this length will be disqualified.

- Send **two** hard copies, to:

END OF STORY
PO BOX 5
MANCHESTER
M60 3GE

by **Monday 31st of May**; entries received after that date, or on e-mail, will be automatically disqualified

- Accompanied by a completed covering sheet, including your name, address, daytime telephone number and the name of the author and short story you have chosen to complete.

You must be:

- Over 16 years of age, as at Monday 31st of May.

- A UK resident.

- Not a professional author.

- Without a conviction which entails current incarceration.

Essential

Please put the following information on a separate sheet of paper at the front of your competition entry.

The BBC will only ever use your personal details for the purposes of administering this competition, and will not publish them or provide them to anyone without your permission. If you would like to know more about the BBC's privacy policy, please visit the website, **www.bbc.co.uk/privacy**

Name
Home address
Home phone number
Mobile number (where applicable)
Daytime contact number
E Mail address (where applicable)
Short story chosen (ie Rankin's, Weldon's)
Word Count

I have read, and agree to abide by the competition rules and entrants agreement.

Signature

Voluntary Information

We would also like to know a little bit more about you, and why you have entered this competition. The following information requests are entirely voluntary and not answering them will not affect the judging of your story. The information will be treated in the strictest confidence.

Your age as of entrance date

Your sex
Male/Female

How did you hear about the competition?
TV Show/website/print
Radio/End Of Story Book/
Other/please specify

Ethnic origin

Asian/Asian British
Black/Black British
Middle/Near Eastern
Mixed Ethnic Group
White
Other/please specify

Do you have ambitions to be a professional writer?

Why have you chosen to enter the competition?

Why did you select the story you have chosen?

Entrant's Agreement

By submitting a story you grant to the BBC a perpetual, royalty-free, non-exclusive, license to sub-edit, publish, make available and distribute your story throughout the world on any BBC media now known or hereafter invented throughout the universe.

In submitting a story, you agree that if you are selected as one of the finalists you will work with the BBC Production team for the production of the forthcoming associated TV series. The finalists must be available for a limited amount of filming, may be required to take part in publicity and be able to travel to UK locations during summer 2004.

The stories can only be submitted by post to the following address:

END OF STORY
PO BOX 5
MANCHESTER
M60 3GE

The BBC does not accept any responsibility for late or lost entries. Proof of sending is not proof of receipt.

- Only one entry will be accepted per person.

- Please make us aware of any past or current convictions.

- No entry can be returned.

- Entries must be within the boundaries of acceptable taste, language and decency.

The entries will be judged by a professional team of readers and experts who will select a short-list of winning entries for each story, on the basis of their originality and appropriateness in providing an ending. The author will make the final decision from the short-list. The BBC's decision is final and no correspondence will be entered into.

All stories may be published on the End of Story website on BBCi.